Little Grey Rabbit's
CHRISTMAS

This edition of
Little Grey Rabbit's Christmas
has been specially abridged

Abridged text copyright © The Alison Uttley Literary Property Trust 1999

First published in Great Britain by William Collins Sons & Co Ltd in 1939
This edition published by HarperCollins*Publishers* in 1999
Original text copyright © The Alison Uttley Literary Property Trust 1939
Illustrations copyright © The Estate of Margaret Tempest 1939, 1999
Illustration on p4 by Mary Cooper.

1 3 5 7 9 10 8 6 4 2

ISBN: 0 00 1983768

The HarperCollins website address is: www.**fire**and**water**.com

Printed in Hong Kong.

60TH ANNIVERSARY EDITION

Little Grey Rabbit's
CHRISTMAS

ALISON UTTLEY *and* MARGARET TEMPEST

Collins

An Imprint of HarperCollins*Publishers*

IT HAD BEEN SNOWING for hours. Hare stood in the garden of the little house at the end of the wood, watching the snowflakes tumbling down like white feathers from the sky.

"Whatever are you doing, Hare?" cried Squirrel, who sat close to the fire. "Come in! You'll catch cold."

"I am catching cold, and eating it too," replied Hare, happily.

"Hare! How long do you think Grey Rabbit will be? What is she doing?" called Squirrel.

"She's at the market, buying Christmas fare for all of us," replied Hare, and he caught an extra large snowflake on his red tongue.

IT WAS GROWING dark when Squirrel and Hare heard the sound of merry voices and the ringing of bells.

They ran to the door, and what should they see but a fine scarlet sledge drawn by two young rabbits, with little Grey Rabbit sitting cosily on the top!

"Oh, Grey Rabbit, what a lovely sledge!" cried Squirrel, rubbing her paws over the smooth sides.

"Grey Rabbit! Our names are on it!" shouted Hare.

"Yes. It's our very own," said Grey Rabbit happily.

T HE NEXT DAY, Squirrel and Grey Rabbit sat on the sledge, and Hare pulled them over the fields until they came to their favourite hill.

Hare sat behind them and away they went down the steep slope. The sledge flew like lightning.

"Whoo-oo-oo!" cried Hare. "Whoops! Whoa!" But the sledge wouldn't stop. At last it struck a molehill and over they all toppled, tumbling head over heels.

Little Fuzzypeg the Hedgehog, carrying a slice of bread and jam for his lunch, came to watch the fun. "I want to toboggan," he said softly, but nobody heard. "Look at *me* toboggan! Watch *me*!"

He made himself into a ball and rolled down the hill, faster and faster.

When he got to the bottom there was no Fuzzypeg to be seen, only an enormous snowball.

"WHAT A BIG snowball!" cried Squirrel. "It's a beauty!" exclaimed Grey Rabbit.

"Help!" squeaked a tiny voice. "Get me out!"

"What's that?" cried Squirrel.

"That's a talking snowball," said Hare. "Isn't that interesting?"

"Help! Help!" shrieked the tiny, faraway voice. "Lemme out!"

"That's like Fuzzypeg's voice," said Grey Rabbit, and she bent over and loosened the caked snow.

Out came the little hedgehog, eating his bread and jam.

"However did you get inside a snowball?" asked Hare.

"I didn't get inside. It got round me," replied Fuzzypeg. "Can I go on your sledge now?"

Hare took the little hedgehog for a ride, but when Fuzzypeg flung his arms round Hare's waist, he sprang shrieking away.

"Never go sledging with a hedgehog," he cried.

So FUZZYPEG ran home and returned with a tea tray. After him came a crowd of rabbits, each carrying a tray, and they all rode helter-skelter down the slope, shouting and laughing.

Squirrel, Hare and little Grey Rabbit took their sledge to Moldy Warp's house.

They gathered holly and mistletoe and Mole helped them to tie their bundle of berries on the sledge. Then they said goodbye and hurried home.

Hare carried the holly and mistletoe indoors. He began to decorate the room, helped by Squirrel. Little Grey Rabbit stood at the table making mince pies.

THE SILVER MOON shone down on the white fields. Up the lane came a little group, carrying rolls of music. They walked up to Grey Rabbit's house, stood in a circle and held up their music to the moonlight.

"Now then, altogether!" cried an important looking rabbit. And they began to sing in small squeaky voices.

"Holly red and mistletoe white,
The stars are shining with golden light,
Burning like candles this Holy Night.
Holly red and mistletoe white."

"**I**T'S CAROL SINGERS!" said little Grey Rabbit, and she flung wide the door.

"Come in!" she cried. "Come in and sing by the fireside. You look frozen with cold."

She took from the fire a mug of primrose wine, and the carollers passed it round. Then they stood by the fire and sang all the songs they knew.

"Now we must be off," they said, when Grey Rabbit had given them hot mince pies. "Good night. Happy Christmas!"

Squirrel, Hare and little Grey Rabbit stood watching them as they crossed the fields.

"I THINK I SHALL take the sledge and toboggan down the hill by moonlight," said Hare.

He seized the cord of the sledge and ran across the fields to the hill.

Then down he swooped, flying like a bird. Suddenly he noticed a dark shadow running alongside him. It was his own shadow, but Hare saw the long ears of a strange monster! "Oh dear!" he cried, and taking to his heels hurried home, leaving the sledge lying in the field.

"Did you come without the sledge?" asked Squirrel. "Hare! I don't believe there was anybody there at all. You ran away from your own shadow! And you've lost our lovely sledge!"

"Better than losing my lovely life," said Hare miserably.
"I suppose we had better go to bed. I don't suppose
Santa Claus will find this house with so much snow
about." But he hung up his furry stocking all the same,
and so did Squirrel.

W HEN ALL was quiet, Grey Rabbit slipped out of bed and filled their stockings with sugar plums and lollipops. Then she ran downstairs to the kitchen, where the fire flickered softly.

She tied together little bunches of holly and made a round ball called a Kissing Bunch, which she hung from a hook on the ceiling.

On Christmas morning, Grey Rabbit didn't wake until Hare burst into her room.

"Grey Rabbit! Wake up! He's been in the night!"

"Who?" cried Grey Rabbit, rubbing her eyes.

"Santa Claus!" exclaimed Hare, dancing up and down. "Quick. Come downstairs and see!"

Grey Rabbit dressed hurriedly and went down to the kitchen.

"Look what he brought me!" said Squirrel, holding out a pair of fur mittens.

"And he gave me a musical box," cried Hare excitedly. "Look at the Kissing Bunch!" he went on. "Let's all kiss under it."

ROBIN THE POSTMAN flew to the door with Christmas cards and a letter.

"It's from Mole," said Hare, twisting it over and over.

"You're reading it upside down, Hare!" cried Squirrel impatiently. She took the letter and read, "Come tonight. Love from Moldy Warp."

"It's a party!" cried Hare. "Oh, Grey Rabbit, say we'll come."

Grey Rabbit wrote on an ivy leaf, "Thank you, dear Moldy Warp."

Then away flew Robin with the leaf in his bag.

 ALL DAY long they enjoyed themselves, playing games, telling stories, pulling tiny crackers, and crunching lollipops. They trooped to the hill to look for the sledge, but it wasn't there. Snow had covered everything.

When it got dark, the three animals wrapped themselves up in warm clothes, and started for Moldy Warp's house, carrying presents for him.

When they got near Mole's house, they saw something glittering. A lighted tree grew by the path.

"Oh," whispered Grey Rabbit. "It's a magical tree."

ON EVERY BRANCH of the little fir tree were lighted candles, and on the ground beneath were bowls of hazelnuts, cakes, tiny jars of honey and bottles of heather ale.

"What do you think of my tree?" asked Moldy Warp, stepping out of the shadows.

"Beau-u-u-tiful," they murmured.

"Is it a fairy tree?" asked Grey Rabbit.

"It's a Christmas tree," said Mole in his soft voice.

"IT'S FOR ALL the animals of the woods and fields. Watch."

Across the snowy fields padded little creatures, all curious to see the glowing tree.

"Help yourselves," cried Mole, waving his arms. "It's Christmas. Eat and drink and warm yourselves."

Then every little creature ate the good food, and drank the sweet honeyed ale.

FROM BEHIND a tree Rat sidled towards Grey Rabbit.

"Miss Grey Rabbit," said he. "I found a scarlet sledge in the field last night, and as your name was on it, I've brought it here for you."

"Oh, thank you, kind Rat," cried Grey Rabbit, clapping her paws. "The sledge is found! Hare! Squirrel! Moldy Warp! Come and see!"

Everyone crowded round to admire the sledge.

On top of it was a fleecy shawl, and Grey Rabbit drew from under it three things. The first was a walking stick, the handle carved in the shape of a hare.

"That must be for me from good Santa Claus," said Hare.

The second was a little wooden spoon with a hazelnut carved in the handle.

"That is certainly mine," said Squirrel and she put it in her pocket.

The third was a wee bone box, and when little Grey

Rabbit opened it, there was a little white thimble inside which exactly fitted her.

"Only one person could make such delicate carvings," said Grey Rabbit.

"And that is Rat," said Squirrel.

"Three cheers for Rat!" they all cried.

THEN SQUIRREL and Grey Rabbit
climbed on the sledge, and Hare drew them
over the snow.

"Good night. A happy Christmas!" they
called to everyone.

Squirrel curled down under the shawl.

But Grey Rabbit sat wide awake, her
thimble was on her finger and her
eyes shone with happiness.

Hare ran swiftly over the frozen snow,
drawing the scarlet sledge towards the little house
at the end of the wood.

Mistletoe white and holly red,
The day is over, we're off to bed.
Tired body and sleepy head,
Mistletoe white and holly red.